A Note to Parents and Caregivers:

With a focus on math, science, and social studies, *Read-it!* Readers support both the learning of content information and the extension of more complex reading skills. They encourage the development of problem-solving skills that help children expand their thinking.

The PURPLE LEVEL presents basic topics and objects using high frequency words and simple language patterns.

The RED LEVEL presents familiar topics using common words and repeating sentence patterns.

The BLUE LEVEL presents new ideas using a larger vocabulary and varied sentence structure.

The YELLOW LEVEL presents more challenging ideas, a broad vocabulary, and wide variety in sentence structure.

The GREEN LEVEL presents more complex ideas, an extended vocabulary range, and expanded language structures.

The ORANGE LEVEL presents a wide range of ideas and concepts using challenging vocabulary and complex language structures.

When sharing a content focused book with your child, read to find out facts and concepts, pausing often to restate and talk about the new information. The realistic story format provides an opportunity to talk about the language used, and to learn about reading to problem-solve for information. Encourage children to measure, make maps, and consider other situations that allow them to apply what they are learning.

There is no right or wrong way to share books with children. Find time to read and share new learning with your child, and pass on the legacy of literacy.

Adria F. Klein, Ph.D.
Professor Emeritus
California State University
San Bernardino, California

Editor: Shelly Lyons
Designer: Abbey Fitzgerald
Page Production: Michelle Biedscheid
Art Director: Nathan Gassman
Associate Managing Editor: Christianne Jones
The illustrations in this book were created with acrylics.

Picture Window Books
151 Good Counsel Drive
P.O. Box 669
Mankato, MN 56002-0669
877-845-8392
www.picturewindowbooks.com

Printed in the United States of America.

All books published by Picture Window Books
are manufactured with paper containing at least
10 percent post-consumer waste.

Library of Congress Cataloging-in-Publication Data
Emerson, Carl.
The autumn leaf / by Carl Emerson ; illustrated by Cori Doerrfeld.
p. cm. — (Read-it! readers: Science)
Summary: The old oak tree in the park explains to Emma and Owen about the
changes that autumn brings.
ISBN 978-1-4048-2624-3 (library binding)
ISBN 978-1-4048-4755-2 (paperback)
[1. Autumn—Fiction. 2. Oak—Fiction. 3. Trees—Fiction.] I. Doerrfeld, Cori, ill.
II. Title.
PZ7.E582Ol 2007
[E]—dc22   2006003386

The Autumn Leaf

by Carl Emerson
illustrated by Cori Doerrfeld

Special thanks to our advisers for their expertise:

Dr. Jon E. Ahlquist, Ph.D.
Department of Meteorology, Florida State University
Tallahassee, Florida

Adria F. Klein, Ph.D.
Professor Emeritus, California State University
San Bernardino, California

PICTURE WINDOW BOOKS
Minneapolis, Minnesota

Old Oak lived in the park.

4

Her leaves took in the sun.

5

But the autumn wind was blowing.

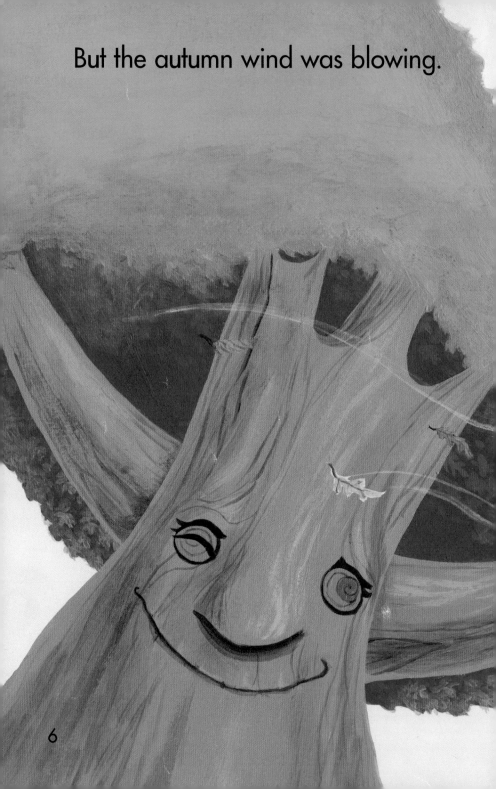

It moved through Old Oak's leaves.

In North America, the season of autumn begins in September and ends in December. The seasons of winter, spring, and summer follow.

Emma and Owen noticed the green leaves were changing.

The leaves turned red and orange.

In autumn, each day has a little less daylight than the one before it.

One day, Emma and Owen went to the park.

They swung from Old Oak's branches.

Emma and Owen sat on the fattest branch.

Orange leaves fell to the ground.

In autumn, leaves don't get enough sunlight, so they change color and fall from the trees.

Suddenly, Emma and Owen noticed the leaves were mostly gone. One last leaf held on.

Another word for autumn is "fall." The season gets this name because the leaves fall from trees in autumn.

Old Oak tried shaking. Old Oak tried leaning.

Old Oak asked the wind to blow.
The leaf just wouldn't drop.

Emma and Owen looked at the little leaf.

It was scared.

Emma had an idea.

Emma and Owen climbed down.

They made a huge leaf pile.

The little leaf watched.

Emma and Owen jumped in. They laughed and played.

"Fall!" they yelled to the little leaf.

The little leaf let go of the branch.

It floated down to the pile of leaves.

The little leaf looked up at Old Oak.
It looked up at Emma and Owen.

"That was fun!" said the little leaf.

Old Oak smiled. She was finally ready for winter.

Fun Fall Activities

You can do many fun things in autumn. Here are some ideas:

- Collect many different kinds of leaves and make a leaf book.

- Visit a local apple orchard to pick apples. While you are there, learn how apple cider and applesauce are made.

- Hold a pumpkin-carving contest in your neighborhood. Ask the adults to be the judges. Make simple ribbons for the winners.

- Make a picture of a tree using leaves and twigs you collect from a real tree.

- Make a nature journal. Write down all of the things you see on your outdoor hikes. Include things like bark rubbings, pressed flowers, and drawings of animals.

- Collect pinecones that have fallen from evergreen trees. Keep them in a warm place until they pop open. Then gather the seeds. Plant the seeds in a small container. Let them grow over the winter. Replant your new trees outside in the spring.

Glossary

autumn—the season after summer and before winter
fall—another name for autumn
season—one of the four parts of the year; winter, spring, summer, and autumn

To Learn More

More Books to Read

Buscaglia, Leo. *The Fall of Freddie the Leaf.* New York: Henry Holt and Co., 2002.

Ehlert, Lois. *Leaf Man.* Orlando, Fla.: Harcourt, 2005.

Frank, John. *A Chill in the Air: Nature Poems for Fall and Winter.* New York: Simon & Schuster Books for Young Readers, 2003.

Knudsen, Michelle. *Autumn is for Apples.* New York: Random House, 2001.

On the Web

FactHound offers a safe, fun way to find Web sites related to topics in this book. All of the sites on FactHound have been researched by our staff.

1. Visit *www.facthound.com*
2. Type in this special code: 1404826246
3. Click on the FETCH IT button.

Your trusty FactHound will fetch the best sites for you!

Look for all of the books in the *Read-it!* Readers: Science series:

Friends and Flowers (life science: bulbs)
The Grass Patch Project (life science: grass)
The Sunflower Farmer (life science: sunflowers)
Surprising Beans (life science: beans)

The Moving Carnival (physical science: motion)
A Secret Matter (physical science: matter)
A Stormy Surprise (physical science: electricity)
Up, Up in the Air (physical science: air)

The Autumn Leaf (Earth science: seasons)
The Busy Spring (Earth science: seasons)
The Cold Winter Day (Earth science: seasons)
The Summer Playground (Earth science: seasons)